SUGAR CRASH

MELINDA DI LORENZO

orca soundings

ORCA BOOK PUBLISHERS

Published in Canada and the United States in 2025 by Orca Book Publishers.

Library and Archives Canada Cataloguing in Publication
Title: Sugar crash / Melinda Di Lorenzo.
Names: Di Lorenzo, Melinda, 1977- author
Series: Orca soundings.
Description: Series statement: Orca soundings
Identifiers: Canadiana (print) 2024045684X | Canadiana (ebook) 20240456858 | ISBN 9781459840249 (softcover) | ISBN 9781459840256 (PDF) | ISBN 9781459840263 (EPUB)
Subjects: LCGFT: Novels.
Classification: LCC PS8607.I23 S84 2025 | DDC jC813/.6—dc23

Library of Congress Control Number: 2024945860

Summary: In this high-interest accessible novel for teen readers, diabetic teen Zoe Harmon races against time and low insulin when she and a classmate have a car accident on a remote mountain road.

Orca Book Publishers is committed to reducing the consumption of nonrenewable resources in the production of our books. We make every effort to use materials that support a sustainable future.

Orca Book Publishers gratefully acknowledges the support for its publishing programs provided by the following agencies: the Government of Canada, the Canada Council for the Arts and the Province of British Columbia through the BC Arts Council and the Book Publishing Tax Credit.

Design by Ella Collier.
Edited by Gabrielle Prendergast.
Cover artwork by krissikunterbunt/Shutterstock.com.

Printed and bound in Canada.

29 28 27 26 • 2 3 4 5

CERTIFIED CANADIAN PUBLISHER

ORCA BOOK PUBLISHERS
orcabook.com

To my parents, for raising me to live fearlessly with T1D, teaching me to advocate for myself, and making sure I always had agency over my own health.

Chapter One

Q: If you were stranded on a deserted island, how would you survive?

A: I wouldn't.

Back when I was in seventh grade, that was the topic for our final project. And yep, that was my full essay.

Our teacher that year was Mr. Flannigan. He was obsessed with survivalist stuff. How to build a shelter from sticks and leaves. How to live off nothing but moss and berries. How to kill a bear with a toothpick. Whatever. None of it mattered to me. Because in seventh grade, I'd just received my official diagnosis. Type 1 diabetes. T1D for short. It means that for the rest of my life, every single day, I have to inject human-made insulin into my body. Well, that or die. So yeah. How would I survive on a deserted island? Like I wrote back then. I wouldn't. Easy peasy answer.

I got an F on that assignment, by the way. Surprise, surprise.

"Oh Zoe," my mom said when she saw it.

She wasn't mad, though. Hard to get pissed off at a twelve-year-old with a life-changing diagnosis like mine.

But that was five years ago. So why am I thinking about all of this now? It's practically ancient history. I'm in twelfth grade. Final semester before graduation. And I think that old teacher, Mr. Flannigan, might even have moved to the forest and started a cult or something. But anyway. Here is the answer. I'm thinking about it because I'm five minutes late and about to fail another English paper. I don't normally care about school, to be honest. My biggest goal is to get it over with. Except I *can't* get it over with if I fail.

So. Here I am. Literally running through the street, trying to make it on time for the school bus. The whole twelfth grade is headed up to the mountains today. We're going on an overnight field trip. A glorified hike. Experiencing nature. Staying in cabins. Blah, blah. And when we're done, we all have to write an essay about the trip. Something about how it relates back to graduating and moving into adult life or whatever. It's worth 20 percent of our grade, and my grade presently sucks. Just like it did back in seventh grade when I was still adjusting to being diabetic. And how does this relate to now? Well, my T1D is the reason I'm late.

It was a classic bottom-out situation. A bit of a

change in my schedule because I didn't have to be at school until after lunch. A not-so-perfect adjustment on my part. Food went in. Insulin went in. Insulin did its job. Food did not. I got the shakes and the sweats and the added hunger that go along with low blood sugar. Cue up snack for correction—juice box, four crackers and a spoonful of peanut butter. Splash in a fifteen-minute wait for that to hit my bloodstream, and I was out the door way later than planned. And here I am, five minutes behind schedule. Actually, more like seven minutes now. Because running with an extra-full stomach does not make me speedy. Plus hiking boots. So...yeah. *Ugh.*

Anyway, I'm going as fast as I can. And finally I hit the corner right before the school parking lot. Which is when I see it. The big yellow school bus. It's already leaving, and it's going in the opposite direction. Turning right when I'm coming in from the left.

"Hey!" I shout. "Wait!"

It's a pretty useless holler. No one can hear me from that far away. I yell again anyway.

"Hey!"

I keep running too. I try to speed up, and I even add some arm flapping. Who knows? Maybe if I look ridiculous enough, it will attract attention. One of the kids in the back of the bus has to turn around, right? But they don't. Or if they do, they don't alert anyone. Right as I reach the parking lot, the bus turns at the end of the block, and its big yellow bus butt disappears from sight.

Breathing hard, I sink down to the sidewalk curb. I'd be cursing up a storm, but my lungs are heaving too much to manage more than a half-hearted "Goddammit."

As if to prove that things can and will get worse, my insulin pump alarms from inside my pocket.

"Shut up," I tell it.

But I shift so that I can pull out the pump anyway. It's second nature. When it blurts an alert, I obey its call. After all, my life does depend on it.

The tiny screen glares up at me with its angry message. *Alert on high.* My pump is attached to a system that monitors my blood sugar, and right now it's not too happy with me.

I wrinkle my nose and clear the alarm. Automatically I debate giving myself a correction dose of insulin. I decide against it. Highs sometimes come after the lows. Like jumping on a trampoline. What goes down must come up. But if I treat it, I might wind up low all over again, and that's the last thing I need right now.

I shove the pump back in my pocket and stare at the end of the street. If I'm hoping for a bus-related miracle, it doesn't come.

With a sigh, I push to my feet and try to come up with a solution. I could text one of my friends on the bus and ask them to beg the driver to turn around. But my two closest friends aren't even in English this semester. One person I do hang out with told me he's skipping, and I had a fight with my other friend last night. So I'm hooped. Plus, everybody who *isn't* a friend—and I'm not exactly Miss Popularity—would be super pissed at me if I held up the trip. How often do we get a chance to avoid an entire day of school like this?

My fingers tap my thigh as my brain keeps working for some other answer.

I guess I could call my mom and ask her for a ride up the mountain. Blame the low blood sugar for my lateness. I mean, it's not like it's a lie. But with five years of diabetes under my belt, she gets annoyed a whole lot easier than she used to.

You have to plan for these things, Zoe. You have to give yourself extra time in case something goes wrong, she would probably say. *Diabetes is a* reason *for lots of things in your life, but you shouldn't use it as an excuse for any of them. Besides which, I can't leave work unless it's an emergency. You know this.*

"Yeah, yeah," I mutter.

Because I do know. My dad left her—left the two of us—high and dry last year. Took off with his secretary, in a perfect cliché. So Mom's paychecks are important and calling her for this would be unfair. Especially if she gave in and showed up.

I swing around to face the school itself. I take a reluctant step toward it. There are a million things I'd rather do than tell the office staff how I missed the bus. But it's looking like my only choice. Other than skipping school, accepting a failing grade and possibly having to repeat English 12 over the summer, that is. I've spent every single weekend for a whole year working at Chuck E. Cheese. Saving money for a trip to Italy. No way am I giving that up.

I take another step, then stop when I spot another twelfth grader.

"Shit," I say under my breath.

Vic Niels.

My worst enemy. And he's headed my way with a sneer on his face.

Chapter Two

It takes me a long second to realize Vic isn't looking at me. He's got his phone in his hand and wireless earbuds in his ears. Whatever's making his lip curl like that, it's not me. It's good news because it gives me a chance to get away before he sees me. Or at least it *should* give me time to go. But I don't move. For some reason, my feet stay frozen while my eyes follow Vic.

What the hell, Zoe?

Seriously. I should take off. On a list of people I don't want to run into, Vic is number one. Maybe he's numbers two, three and four too. I'll even give him spot five if he wants it.

I hate him.

I hate the way his blond hair hangs in his eyes like he's some kind of rock star.

I hate how he's grown three inches this year so now he's over six feet tall.

I hate knowing he's good at math and bad at poetry and is afraid of heights.

But what I hate most is that he used to be my best friend.

Oh, is that *why we're still standing here?* my brain asks me. *You wanna go back in time?*

I shake my head a tiny bit. I've spent the last five years trying to forget that Vic and I were ever close. Mostly by avoiding him. I've gotten pretty good at it.

If I see him in the hallway, I duck into a bathroom. Or I find an interesting wall to stare at. Or pretend to vomit. No word of a lie, I did that one time last year.

But here I am now, just watching Vic come in my direction. Worse, my eyes follow him as he swings left and heads for the parking lot.

If you're not gonna leave, you could at least bend down and pretend to tie up your boot or something, I tell myself.

I don't do it, though. I stare instead. I watch him as he walks toward his car. It distracts me for a second. The car, I mean. It's painted flat black, except for the driver's-side door. That's red. One time I overheard some tenth grader talking about how awesome the tires are. I remember wondering who the hell cares that much about pieces of rubber.

I narrow my eyes, thinking about it.

Vic claims he basically built the car himself. But his dad is a mechanic, so I know better. Vic idolizes his dad. Or he did back when we were friends. I don't care that he got help, though. Why would I? But it pisses me off that Vic *lies* about it.

Giant Turd. It's my favorite insult, and I think it fits just fine.

But didn't Vic come up with it in the first place? my annoying brain asks.

Grudgingly I admit that he did. His mom caught him calling someone an "a-hole." That was the term she used. And she told Vic to get creative instead. He came up with Giant Turd, capitalized, and it stuck around. He can have the credit for it because *one* of us is honest. That doesn't mean I won't use the words against him.

Giant, Giant Turd.

For some reason, I still haven't looked away from him. It's not until he digs his keys from his pocket that I catch on to why my feet haven't moved.

His car. Duh, Zoe.

Some of the kids got permission to drive themselves. Vic could be one of them. And if he *is* driving, he might be my ticket out of here. More importantly, he might be my ticket up the mountain.

My mouth opens before I can stop it. "Hey!"

Vic doesn't seem to hear me. He does drop his keys on the ground, though, and I snort.

Nice work.

I take a step closer and call out again. "Earth to Vic!"

There's still no sign that he can hear me. Then I remember.

The headphones.

I open my mouth, then close it as something occurs to me. Maybe Vic not hearing me is a cosmic sign that I shouldn't even ask him. It's a pretty wild idea anyway. Being stuck in a car with my former best friend for, like, four hours wouldn't be fun.

Understatement of the year.

My fingers tighten at my sides. I'll find some other way to get there. One that doesn't involve Vic Niels. If that doesn't work, I'll beg my English teacher not to fail me. If I can avoid Vic by pretending to puke, I can convince a teacher to forgive a grade, can't I?

I'm about to walk up to the school, but my phone buzzes in my pocket. I stay where I am and yank it out. I'm hoping for a miracle. Some excuse that'll get me out of the field trip altogether. I get the opposite. It's an email. A snarky one from my English teacher.

Ms. Harmon.

This is a final reminder that if you don't complete this project, you will not receive a passing grade in English 12. Zero exceptions. Failing means you don't graduate on time.

Sincerely,

Mrs. Sawyer.

"Dammit," I say.

When I look up from my phone, I can see that Vic has noticed me at last. In fact, he's staring at me. I have an urge to tell him to take a picture if he's so obsessed with me. But I keep it in. Barely.

I head toward him and try to smile.

"What's wrong with you?" Vic asks once I'm right in front of him.

Clearly my smile is a fail. I give him the basics anyway.

"I missed the bus," I say. "Low blood sugar. But if I don't go on the trip and write the essay, I'll fail the class."

"Sorry to hear that," he replies.

Vic isn't sorry at all. I can tell by the flatness in his voice. It's possible he'd be *happy* if I failed. *Giant Turd.* But I pretend not to notice.

"Thanks," I tell him instead. "Are you driving up?"

"Why?" he asks.

I force my smile to get wider. It makes my jaw hurt. *You really need me to say it, don't you?*

Out loud, I'm polite. "If you're driving, could I score a ride with you?"

"Seriously?"

I shrug. "You're literally my only option, Vic. Do you really think I *want* to ride in your deathmobile?"

"You're selling this well," he replies. "My car is totally safe. My dad helped me build it."

So I guess he's not lying about that, then. I shove aside the thought and say, "Look, I'm desperate. And I'll pay you twenty bucks."

"Jesus." He flicks his hair out of his eyes. "I'll take you, and you can keep your money. But there's one thing, okay?"

I try not to roll my eyes. Of *course* Vic has a condition. But I'm going to agree to whatever it is. No other choice, remember?

"Name it," I say.

"No diabetes talk."

Chapter Three

My grammy has this saying. *Spitting mad.* I've always thought it was cute. Like, an old-person way of saying "pissed off." But at that second, when Vic warns me off talking about my *diabetes*, I get it.

I want to spit. Mostly words.

Fuck you, Vic, would do nicely.

In fact, I'm so mad that spitting seems like the only thing I *could* do. My body is too stiff to throw a punch. My brain is too shocked to say anything clever. And I need the ride too much to just walk away.

Spitting mad. Yeah, that's me right now, Grammy.

But I'm not going to give Vic the satisfaction of knowing it.

I take a couple of breaths. I meet his eyes. Then I nod and walk around to the other side of his car like it's no big deal. Do I catch a flicker of disappointment on his face? I think I do. I hope so, actually. I might need him, but Vic doesn't deserve this to be easy.

I beat him into the car, and by the time he's in front of the steering wheel, I've already buckled up.

He doesn't say anything, and that's fine by me. Better still, he cranks the radio. It's blaring out some serious '90s tunes so loud we couldn't talk even if we wanted to. Also fine. I'll gladly take Kurt Cobain's voice over Vic Niels's voice any day.

No diabetes talk, my big toe.

We pull out of the parking lot, and in minutes we're on the highway. We get stuck in traffic because of course we do. The cars basically inch along. But I keep my attention on the window so I won't just sit and glare at Vic. It doesn't stop my thoughts from coming in like darts.

Why does Vic care whether I talk about my diabetes anyway? It's not like it's even something I normally do. Who wants to hear about injecting insulin, and blood sugars? I save that for my doctors. I don't even complain about it to my mom very often. Back in tenth grade, I used to sometimes hang out with this girl Ruby. We were friends for six months before she even found out that I'm T1D. She was shocked when I treated a high blood sugar. I was shocked that she was shocked.

I mean, yeah, okay. Diabetes can dominate my life sometimes. Like today, for example. Managing it is kind of like having a part-time job. Except instead of getting paid, I get to keep living.

But again...why does *Vic* care?

I take a quick look at him from the corner of my eye. He's focused on the road. Which is a good thing, because the traffic has gotten even worse and it's raining pretty hard right now. The droplets hit the windshield faster than the wipers can clear them.

I take out my phone and pretend to text. Actually, I type up real texts—long rants about Vic and his Giant Turd status—then delete them. The last thing I need is for any of my friends to know who I'm with. I complained about Vic one time to this girl Charlotte, and she told three other girls. They bugged me for a month. Called him my boyfriend. Ugh. Such babies.

Never again, I vowed.

I can keep feelings to myself. I drop my phone into my bag so I'm not tempted to text anyway. But my brain continues to work.

Like I said before, Vic and I used to be tight. We live on the same block. Have the same favorite food. Both hate black licorice. We once tried to convince our moms to let us get matching tattoos. The begging went on for months. We were ten. Honestly, something else that I don't tell anyone *ever*? Vic was my first kiss too. We planned it, and it happened a few days before I found out about being diabetic. We've never talked about it, and I don't even like to *think* about it. I sure wish it wasn't on my mind now.

Why *is* it on my mind? *Gah*. He's a Giant Turd, and he shouldn't even have lips.

I press my forehead to the window in case Vic is watching me. God knows I don't need *him* thinking about that kiss. With any luck, he's forgotten.

It's not like it matters anyway. After I got diabetes, all the fun stuff stopped. I'd go to Vic's house, and his mom would tell me he was sick. Five minutes later I'd see him on his bike in the back alley. If I tried to talk to him, he'd pedal away. After a while I gave up trying. Why waste my time, right?

I've always thought he started avoiding me because it was suddenly weird to be close friends with a girl. Especially a girl he'd kissed. But what if I've been wrong all this time? What if he stopped being friends with me because of my diabetes?

That makes no sense, Zoe. Unfriending someone because of diabetes?

I'm so caught up in my own head that I don't realize how long we've been on the road until I spot a sign. It's big. Like, huge. In bold letters, it says *Next Stop, Waverly Mountain!* And a bright-green arrow is under the words, pointing to the right.

But we're driving *past* it.

For the first time, I speak up, lifting my question over the music. "Um. Hello? Did you just miss our turn?"

Vic doesn't even look at me when he answers. "No."

"Yeah, you did." I practically have to yell.

"No, I didn't," he says.

I reach over and turn down the volume.

"There was a sign back there," I tell him.

"I know," he replies. "But we're running, like, an hour behind, so we're taking a shortcut."

"How can it be a shortcut if it's *past* where we want to go?"

"It just is."

"If you're going to murder me and throw me in a ravine, just tell me," I say.

Suddenly he looks like he's trying not to laugh. I wait for it. It's been a long time since I've heard him make a happy sound anywhere near me. But when he answers, it's in a serious voice.

"Do you remember Mr. Flannigan?" he asks. "From, like, seventh grade?"

I nod, even though it's weird how I was *just* thinking about the same teacher.

"The survival guy," I say.

"Right. Well, he took the class on a hike up here. He drove that bright-blue bus, and he took a back way. *Past* the sign," Vic explains. "It cut fifteen minutes off the trip."

"Wait. Where was *I*?" I wonder aloud. "I didn't get that—" I stop as I suddenly remember. The hike was the same week that I got my diagnosis. I'm dangerously close to "diabetes talk," and Vic's jaw is tight. Any trace of the laugh is gone. He turns up the stereo again, but right before the music comes back on, my insulin pump blurts an alarm. It's like it *knows* he doesn't want me to mention it.

I don't have to look to know what it says, either. *Approaching low limit.* And now that the alarm has gone off, I feel the low blood sugar myself. My hands tingle a tiny bit. My head is kind of soupy. Like I just woke up from a terrible sleep. If I don't eat soon, it'll get worse. I'll start to sweat and shiver and get weak.

Wordlessly I unbuckle myself so I can grab my backpack from where I set it in the back seat. I dig around until I find a sugar tab and a granola bar. I pop the first thing into my mouth like candy, which it kind of is. Then I eat the granola bar like I'm starving, which is how I'll feel if I wait.

I stay silent as I finish treating the low blood sugar. But mentally I'm daring Vic to say something about it. He's quiet too, though. A quick look his way tells me he's focused on the road. Again that's a good thing. Those raindrops from a while back? They're snowdrops now. Not quite flakes but not just water anymore either.

A few minutes pass.

The snow gets thicker. Vic even slows down.

I'm feeling both better and worse. My blood sugar is going back up to normal, but my anxiety about the weather is making my stomach churn. Isn't it supposed to be close to summer? I know we're in the mountains, but this is ridiculous. I packed *shorts* in my bag.

I can barely see through the windshield now. The granola bar is a lump in my gut.

Ugh.

I open my mouth. I'm going to ask Vic if he thinks we should stop. Or maybe I'm going to tell him that *I* think we should. But I don't get a chance. Before a single word can form, Vic hits the brakes for some reason.

The car skids. The windshield clears for a moment. Just long enough to draw a scream from my throat. We're headed straight for a cliff. But I hardly have a chance to process what's about to happen before my body jerks forward. I forgot to buckle up my seat belt after grabbing my bag, and my head meets the dashboard. Everything goes black.

Chapter Four

We crash. Of course we crash. It's the only thing that can happen when a car goes over a cliff. But, thankfully, I miss it. I faint before we hit.

I don't get to see us smack into a tree.

I don't have to hear the deafening blow of metal crunching on impact.

I don't watch the passenger door fly off or feel myself get thrown from the car.

Nope. None of that. One second, I'm out. The next

second, I'm pulling my eyes open and staring up at the sky.

Panic zaps at me.

My pulse jumps in my veins, going twice as fast as it should.

I order myself to stay calm because freaking out won't do any good.

Slowly I inhale and pretend not to notice how cold the air is. Then I exhale and ignore the way I can see the breath leaving my lips. I try to sit up so I can make sense of things, but I'm pinned in place. Something is holding me down. My pulse does another quick dance. Why am I stuck?

"Chill out, Zoe." I say it out loud just so I can hear a sound.

Because it really is quiet. Like, eerily so. Horror-movie territory. Why do I feel like I'm about to be eaten by a killer clown?

And Vic. Where's Vic?

If anyone deserves to be eaten by a killer clown, it's him, not me.

"Vic?" I call.

When I don't get an answer, I lift my hands and feel around until I find what's pressed to my chest. It's a thick tree branch. I shove it aside, and I take a few more breaths. And this time, when I try to sit up, I succeed. But it hurts. Everything hurts. My head. My legs and arms. I swear, even my teeth hurt. They're starting to chatter, too, which doesn't help.

"Vic?" I say again.

I look around, trying to get a feel for the place. Most of what I see is trees. Lots and lots of green and brown. Snow kind of dots the ground, but it's not falling from the sky anymore. There are some big rocks not too far away. Mountainy stuff in the distance.

I frown and chew on my bottom lip for a second. What's missing?

Duh, Zoe. The car. Which is probably where your bestie, good ole Vic, is too.

Still aching all over, I push to my feet. Then I freeze. Now that I'm up, I have a view of the other side of the big rocks. I can see the car. And yeah, Vic's there. He's still strapped into the driver's seat, and the car's windshield is shattered. A broken, jagged branch is only a few inches from his chest. If his seat belt had been undone, like mine was, that branch would have gone straight through his body. He'd be dead. No doubt about it.

"Vic?" I say, moving closer. "Can you hear me?"

When I'm almost beside him, I see that his eyes are shut.

Maybe he is *dead,* a little voice in my head says.

My heart thuds. I stop walking. But I refuse to believe it.

"Uh-uh," I say under my breath. "You are *not* allowed to be dead. You can't just drive me off a cliff and then die. You need to be alive so I can kill you myself."

I push myself to keep going. I step over to him and put my hand on his shoulder.

"Vic?" I say it quietly the first time and louder the next. "Vic!"

He groans, and my shoulders sag. He's alive. *Thank you, universe.* But his eyes stay closed.

That's okay, I tell myself. *I'll just find my phone and call for help. I'll tell him to go to hell after we're safe.*

I start searching. It should be easy enough. I left my phone in my bag, and my bag is a bright shade of orange. In fact, it should be harder *not* to find it. But after a minute of looking, I still see no sign of it.

Where did it go?

My heart taps a *really* uncomfortable beat in my chest. I have to swallow twice. Except all that does is make me realize I'm thirsty.

"Crap," I say, distracted.

Because thirst for a T1D can mean high blood sugar. And all my supplies are in the same bag as my phone.

Anxiously I reach my hand to my pocket and feel for my pump. It's there. I exhale, long and hard. Then I make myself pull out the pump. I'm legit terrified that it's going to be broken. How long would I last without it?

Don't think about that, I tell myself. *Besides which, you're going to be out of this before it even matters.*

I tap the center button on the pump, and when it lights up, I realize my lungs are on fire. I forgot to breathe in. I do it now, releasing the pressure as I examine my literal lifeline.

Everything looks fine. No cracks, not even in the plastic case. The tubing that goes from the pump to my body is properly in place. The home screen tells me that my blood sugar is good too. My pump has kept me in range through it all.

Being bionic for the win.

I shove the pump back into my pocket.

Forget diabetes—I'm probably lucky I didn't get eaten by a bear.

Where are the rescue guys? The ones with helicopters and whatever. I wonder how long it takes for them to notice a crash like ours. I scan the sky like they're going to appear. But maybe Vic's shortcut ruined any hope of that. Or maybe they'll think we took off on purpose or something.

Vic groans again. He mumbles something that might be words, and relief hits me hard. He's not my favorite person, but I don't want him to die.

"Are you complaining? I hope you're not complaining," I say. "Because if you are..."

But when I turn around, my irritation zaps away, and my eyes go wide. The car is on *fire.*

Chapter Five

The orange flames are small and brighter than my backpack. They flicker up from a spot inside the crushed front end of the car. And they hold my attention for way too long.

Um, hello? my brain finally says. *Are we just gonna watch it burn? I mean, we don't like Vic, but didn't we just decide it's better if he's alive?*

I jump forward, looking for the best way to get him out. Because, despite his groans, he still isn't awake. He won't be of any help.

Seat belt, I tell myself. *Get him out of the seat belt.*

"Right. Yeah. Okay."

I go for the obvious. I grab the door handle and pull. When it doesn't budge, I step back and let out my own groan. The whole side of the car is crushed. It looks like an accordion.

I need to get to Vic another way.

My eyes find the other side of the car. That door is missing, which explains how I fell out. Even so, that side is no more help than Vic is, because it's pressed hard to the trunk of a giant tree.

Now my eyes find the broken windshield. Then they go to the hood and its cozy little fire that will probably make the car blow up soon.

So hurry up, Zoe.

I flex my hands, take a couple of breaths and climb onto the small bit of hood that hasn't been destroyed. My instinct is to move slowly. Carefully. You know, to stop myself from sure death. But I can feel the heat from the flames, and it makes me go fast instead.

Sweating already, I crawl closer to Vic. My sweatshirt catches on bits of broken glass as I maneuver through the windshield.

"You're going to be buying me a new hoodie too," I say, leaning in to find the seat-belt buckle.

Even if Vic could hear me, my words are muffled by the fact that my face is pressed to his stomach. But at least he smells nice.

Yeah, 'cause that's what matters now. I fumble around a bit more.

My fingers finally find the metal bit, and I press down. There's a satisfying *click*, and the seat belt zips away from Vic's body.

I lean back. Now what?

He's not a small dude. I'm not a big chick. How am I going to get him out of there? Even if I manage to get him through the windshield, I'll probably drop him on myself. Then I'll suffocate. The car and

Vic will blow up. Our bodies will fuse together, and people will think we died making out. Just what I need.

"Zoe?" Vic says weakly.

I refocus on him. "Oh, thank the sweet baby Jesus."

"What's happening?" he asks.

"We're having ice cream in the park," I reply, heavy on the sarcasm.

Vic's eyebrows come together in a frown. He looks like he thinks I might've meant it, and I feel a bit guilty.

"Come on, man," I say. "We were in a crash. I'm trying to get you out of the car before it explodes."

"Well, damn," he replies weakly.

"Give me your hands," I order. "And watch out for the fire."

His eyes widen. "Fire?"

"Never mind," I say. "Just hurry."

Vic groans a bit more, but he listens. His fingers close on mine, and I pull. He pushes. I move back until my feet find the ground. Together we force him through the windshield. His stomach hits the hood, and he slides forward and lands on his hands and knees.

"Very graceful," I say, stepping back from the car.

Vic grunts, pushes to his feet and moves closer to me. Then he seems to think better of it and sinks to the ground again.

"You okay?" I ask.

"No," he replies. "I was just knocked out in a car accident when I was expecting ice cream."

My heart does one of its nervous jumps, but I roll my eyes. "Are you okay in, like, relative terms, I mean."

"I'm not dead."

"Hey, we have something in common. I'm not dead either."

Now Vic rolls *his* eyes. "Very funny."

The car makes a noise, and we both look toward it. The flames aren't bigger, but they've spread. I take another uneasy step back.

"It probably won't blow up," Vic says after a second. "It'll probably just burn like that for a while."

"Probably?" I repeat.

"I'm pretty sure," he replies.

"Oh, good. Pretty sure is *so* much better than probably."

But I do feel better. Vic knows cars. His *probably* is better than most people's *absolutely.*

In my pocket, my insulin pump chimes. *Alert before low.* Again I don't have to check. Any second, I'll start feeling the drop too. And I don't have my bag, so I don't have my food.

I steal a glance at Vic. He's looking away, maybe annoyed. But I can't even be bothered to care. I move away from him, scanning the area around the car.

C'mon, backpack. Where are you?

I walk over to the nearest bushes and peer into them. A slow blink hits me. Yep, the blood sugar drop is rearing its pain-in-the-butt head.

I work harder, bending over and digging around.

"What are you doing?" Vic asks.

"Looking for my bag," I say without turning around.

"Are you kidding? It's just a purse."

"It's not a purse at all," I reply, still looking. "It's a backpack. And even if it *was* a purse, I'd still have to find it."

"Don't you think we have more important stuff to do?" he asks.

"No, we don't. And I'm not going anywhere or doing anything else until I have it. So suck it, Vic."

"Jesus, Zoe. Come on."

"Look," I say. "My bag has all my diabetic stuff in it. And I know you banned me from talking about that, but I'd like to stay alive. Sorry if that's not what *you* want, Vic."

Unexpectedly, tears burn my eyes. It hits me. I could die. I really could. And even though it's kind of my reality every day, it's never been quite *this* real before. Not ever.

Chapter Six

I refuse—100 percent *refuse*—to let Vic see that I'm crying. He doesn't deserve my feelings. No way do I want him to know how scared I am.

I stomp a bit farther away and start digging through some other bushes. I dig into my pocket in case I have something stashed there. All I find is a metallic gum wrapper and a wad of receipts that came from God knows where.

"Hey," Vic says.

His voice is so close that I jump. And my jump is in the wrong direction, so I bang into him. His hands land on my shoulders to steady me, and I have the weirdest urge to press myself into his chest. To get some comfort and smell his good smell or whatever. I'm even a little sad when he lets me go.

"I don't want you to die," Vic says.

"Gee, thanks." My sarcasm sounds weak, even to my own ears.

"What do you need?" he asks.

"Food. I'm low."

"Will this help?" He reaches into his pocket and pulls out an extra-sugary protein bar.

I nod. "Yes."

"Take it," he says.

"Are you sure?" I reply.

"Are you seriously asking me that?" He lifts one eyebrow, and I remember he used to do that all the time when we were little kids.

Another weird pang hits my chest. What is *wrong* with me? Crying? Wanting to hug Vic? *Ugh.* I'm going to go ahead and blame the low blood sugar. I take the protein bar and scarf down the first half of it.

Vic shakes his head. "I don't get it."

"Get what?" I ask.

"This is the second time you've been low since we left the school," he replies.

Anger wants to surge through me. He's being a *total* Giant Turd. We left the school hours ago. I haven't had a meal. And part of the reason I'm low is because of him. Helping him get out of the car was a workout, so I burned energy. But it's not like it's the first time someone has said something like this to me. I got kicked off the track team for dropping low. I got asked to leave a play because of having my own food with me. And besides that, being mad when I have low blood sugar is too much effort, so I just shrug.

I finish the protein bar, find a tree and plunk myself down in front of it. I lean against the trunk to wait for my blood sugar to go up. And I make sure not to look at Vic. But I can hear him anyway. He's moving around. Snapping branches. Making annoyed noises and cursing to himself. I wish he'd shut up, so I close my eyes to block it out. And finally he stops. His feet tap along the dirt and rocks, and I *know* he's standing in front of me. I pretend not to notice.

He lets out a loud sigh and says, "Here."

I open my eyes because I'm not a *complete* baby. And Vic is holding my backpack. For a second I'm stoked to see it. Eager to have my stuff back, I lean forward and take the bag from him. But my excitement doesn't last. It's empty. No diabetic supplies. No food. No phone. It's probably spread out all over the forest, and there's zero chance I'll find it now.

"Great," I mutter.

Then, as if to prove things can always get worse, a drop of slushy rain lands in the middle of my forehead.

"Sorry," Vic says.

I fight the need to ask him which thing he's apologizing for. There are so many to choose from. Is it the crash? The stuff about my diabetes? Is he saying sorry about the rain, or maybe just about being a total dickwad in general? But when I get a better look at him, I stop.

Vic's got leaves stuck to his hair. He's really pale, and there's a big bruise on his forehead. He's kind of holding his side, like it hurts. And he *did* make an effort to get my bag.

"I don't want you to die," he adds for the second time.

He meets my eyes, and I can see he means it. Which should maybe go without saying. Who wants someone else to die? Like, for real? But it seems almost like he *extra* means it or something.

When we stopped being friends, I felt *like part of me died,* I'm tempted to say with extra-dramatic flair. *Doesn't that count?*

But it's a bit too close to the truth. My world imploded, at least a little. Diabetes. My dad leaving. Losing Vic.

"Any chance you still have your phone?" I ask instead.

He reaches into his pocket, but he's shaking his head. Yeah, he's got the phone, but its whole screen is gone, and all the electronic stuff is exposed. Hopeless city.

We're both quiet for a few seconds. The snowy rain picks up even more, and some wind joins it. It's blasting my skin in a way that makes me think of hypothermia. I shiver. The sky seems to be getting darker fast too.

"We should find some shelter," Vic says.

"Are you gonna build one from sticks and mud?" I ask.

I'm only half joking. I'm already freezing cold, and I'd gladly take sticks and mud at the moment. Maybe Vic was paying better attention to our survival-obsessed seventh-grade teacher.

"If I have to," he says.

Vic puts out his hand to help me up, and I decide to take it. We're stuck here together, and I can play nice for a bit. His fingers are way warmer than I expect them to be. They feel nice. Strong and reassuring. It gives me a prickle of hope. Maybe the car fire will burn long and slow like he said, and we can use it to stay warm. Or maybe it will attract attention from someone looking for us. But as Vic lets go of my hand, he also speaks up. And it's like he just read my mind and wants to personally wreck my hope.

"The rain'll probably put the fire out before anyone realizes we're gone," he says. "If that happens, there won't be enough heat or smoke for the search-and--rescue thermal equipment to pick up on it."

I want to argue, but my pump alarms right then. I see Vic's jaw tighten, and I swallow and look away from him.

I do not *need to feel guilty about this,* I tell myself as I pull my pump from my pocket. *I'm the one who has to get jabbed with needles. I'm the one who lives with this. Vic is just some jerk who doesn't want to talk about it.*

But my thoughts slide away when I see the pump's screen. It's telling me I need to refill it.

Oh no.

My brain is buzzing. I have ten units of insulin left. Five hours' worth.

That's if I don't get high blood sugar, and if I don't eat. Not that we have food. But sometimes highs come from stress. And I think being stranded on the side of a mountain qualifies as stressful.

Maybe I can dial back the insulin delivery a bit. Make it last longer. But not *too* much longer, or I might as well have none coming in at all.

And I'll be okay for a while if I do run out. For how long, I have no idea. A few hours? One time my tubing got pulled out and I didn't know. I *think* it took about two hours before I started to feel gross. But it was really gross. So much puke.

Vic's voice cuts in suddenly, yanking me out of my thoughts and pukey memories. "What's the problem now?" he asks, his annoyance shining through like a flashing sign.

There's no point in keeping it to myself.

"I need to get off the mountain," I state.

"You and me both," he replies.

I shrug. "Sure. But only one of us is going to run out of insulin in five hours if we don't get rescued."

Chapter Seven

I have zero intention of waiting for Vic to answer. Who cares if he doesn't agree? Who cares if he doesn't understand and doesn't *want* to understand? I don't want to hear it. I spin away, ready to take off into the woods. But Vic's hand lands on my elbow.

"Dude, hang *on*," he says.

I shake off his grip. "What do you want?"

"If you think we should hike down, we can hike down," he replies. "But everyone knows your best shot at getting found is staying in one place."

I lift my chin. "*Everyone* isn't diabetic."

"Do you think maybe you're overreacting?"

"Fuck–"

"Yeah, I know. Fuck me. Or fuck off. Or whatever."

I grind my teeth together. Because maybe I *am* overreacting. But it's only for the current moment. If I don't overreact now, I'll regret it a few hours from now. And I won't be able to change it. But again, I'm not going to explain any of that to Vic.

To the guy who gave you his protein bar and found your backpack, you mean?

I ignore my conscience. Two nice gestures don't erase five years of zero contact.

"I don't expect you to get it," I say. "I'm not even asking you to try. But there's a good chance they're not even looking for us yet. They could think we're skipping. And if we wait, then I might be screwed. Like, personally."

"Okay, but can you just listen for a sec, Zoe?" he asks.

I grind my teeth harder and answer him through the clench. "Fine."

He takes a deep breath and reels off a bunch of stuff that makes too much sense. It's going to get dark before all that long. There could be animals. It's cold. It'll be even colder soon. The weather is garbage. We haven't even searched the car to see if there's anything useful inside. We don't know for sure they haven't started looking for us. Vic skips class a bit, but not often enough that they wouldn't notice if he didn't show up. Plus, they're expecting him. He drove today only because he had a dentist appointment. When he doesn't show up, they'll call his mom.

I notice he doesn't mention *me* as being missed, but I can't argue with it. I skip at least one class per week. And since I wasn't on the bus, they probably thought I'd just peaced out on the whole trip. My mom, on the other hand, will just assume I am where I said I'd be.

“But,” Vic says at the end of his speech, “if none of that’s going to make you want to wait it out, then I think we should go somewhere else.”

“Like where?” I reply. “The nearest cave full of hyenas?”

“We don’t have hyenas here,” he says with exaggerated patience.

I cross my arms over my chest. “Fine. Cave full of coyotes then.”

“I’m talking about heading for the road, Zoe.” He points up, and I follow the direction of his finger.

“You want to go *up*?” I ask. “What happened to *down*?”

His hand drops. “Not literally up. But if we try to get to the closest stretch of road instead of all the way to the bottom of the mountain...”

I push my lips together. But as much as I hate to admit it, he’s right. If we can get to the road, we stand a better chance of being found. Even late at night, someone could drive by and see us. Plus, it’s probably faster to find our way there than to head down. The bottom is miles away.

"If it's bugging you that much, you can take credit for the idea," Vic says.

"I'm not a five-year-old," I reply.

"No kidding. Five-year-old you *definitely* would've wanted credit."

I lift each hand and give him two middle fingers. But if I'm being honest, my heart's not in it. And he might even be right about five-year-old me.

"Okay," I say, sighing extra loudly. "Let's try it your way."

"Car first, then road?" he asks.

"Sure. Why not? Maybe we'll get lucky."

But while we've been arguing, the car fire has spread. Made itself at home there despite the weather. And Vic was right yet again, dammit. No explosion. Just a slow burn that makes it impossible for us to even attempt to look through the vehicle.

"Well, that's that," Vic says.

He sounds so disappointed that I feel bad. The car probably meant a lot to him. Not every twelfth grader has their own vehicle. And as far as I know, Vic's is the only one that was hand built. I don't even feel the need to say something sarcastic to him like, *Maybe your next car won't be quite so ugly.*

"You wanna hang out until it's over?" I ask.

He shakes his head. "No. It doesn't matter."

"Maybe the rain will put it out, like you said before," I reply.

"It will. Just not quick enough to save it."

Impulsively I reach out and squeeze his hand. He squeezes back, holding on tightly, and for about five seconds, it doesn't feel weird. We watch the flames and hold hands and it's *la-di-da.* Of course, when *six* seconds have passed, it gets super awkward. But it's almost worse when we let go at the same time. Like our hands are on fire instead of the car.

"We should go," I say, glad the storm makes it dark enough to cover how red my cheeks must be.

"Yep." Vic straightens his shoulders, shakes his head, then starts off.

I have to scramble to catch up, and for a second I'm annoyed again. I'm even *more* annoyed when he tells me in a bossy voice which direction we have to walk. He's such a know-it-all. But I forget about my irritation as we move farther and farther into the woods. Maybe he really was paying better attention to the survival teacher than I was back in seventh grade.

It's so quiet that every little sound seems twice as loud as it should be. An owl screeches, and I jump. Some small creature—a rabid squirrel comes to mind—chitters angrily. I move faster just in case.

But after maybe fifteen minutes, I realize that Vic's fallen behind, instead of me, and I spin around. I turn just in time to see him pulling his jacket down over his stomach. But why did he have it lifted up in the first place?

"What are you doing?" I ask.

"Nothing." He says it far too quickly.

"You're a bad liar, Vic," I reply. "You always have been."

He rolls his eyes, but he also grimaces.

My eyes drop to his stomach. A bad feeling slithers along my shoulders.

"Show me," I order.

"It's nothing."

"Show me!"

With a sigh, he lifts up the bottom of his jacket. He's got a white T-shirt underneath. And it's stained dark red with blood.

Chapter Eight

I want to give Vic the hardest shove *ever.* Then maybe a punch in the gut. But his gut is kind of close to the blood, so I just clench my hands into fists and suppress a scream.

Are you mad or scared? my jerk of a subconscious asks.

I'm both, obviously. But I tell myself to shut up, and I focus on Vic.

"You need to sit down," I say.

“I’m fine,” he replies.

“Didn’t I already tell you what a bad liar you are?” I ask.

“Yeah. Five seconds ago.”

“Which means it’s still true. Lift up your whole shirt.”

“If you’re trying to get me naked...” He lifts a suggestive eyebrow.

I can’t even make a disgusted face. “Just lift up the shirt, Vic.”

He sighs, then does as he’s told. And my breath sticks in my throat, and I forget about my low-insulin problem. Vic’s got a huge gash just below his ribs. It looks bad. Like, *so* bad. It’s as long as my hand. An inch wide. The edges of the cut are jagged and choppy.

My head goes to that tree branch that was in the car. The one I thought might kill him. It did this. I’m sure of it.

"I'm fine, Zoe," Vic says again.

He's not, though. His words are too soft. And his face is kind of sweaty, and I don't think it's just from hiking through the trees.

"We need to find a place to rest so we can clean you up," I say.

I wait for him to argue. But he doesn't. And that makes my heart drop pretty much to my toes. He's not fighting with me, so he's gotta be even worse off than I thought.

"How far do you think you can walk?" I ask.

"As far as I need to," he replies.

Not far at all, I think as he shifts uncomfortably in place.

I turn away from him to scan the area around us. The forest makes it too dark to see very far, but I spot a huge tree trunk. It's as tall as I am and hollow. Biggest one I've ever seen. It's got enough room for both Vic and me to sit inside of it. Plus, there are some branches hanging above it, so we'll have a bit of shelter too.

I point. "There."

"Okay," he agrees.

Still not arguing. *Not good.* But at least he walks on his own to the tree trunk without any trouble.

"Wait here for a second, okay?" I say as he gets settled in. "I'm going to find something I can use to clean that cut."

"Oh, you're going to hit the nearest pharmacy?" he says.

"Shut up." But for once, I don't mean it.

I step away from Vic and the tree trunk so I can look around again. I'm careful not to get too far away, though. The last thing I need is to get lost. It's the last thing he needs too.

Thankfully, I spy a bush just a few feet from us. It's got wide leaves that curve up, creating the perfect place for rain to collect. I hurry over to pick some, but I stop myself as a new worry occurs to me.

What if it's poison ivy?

I bite my lip. I swear there's some trick to remembering what poison ivy looks like. But I was only a Girl Scout for about five minutes, and my brain isn't working all that great right now.

Maybe Vic knows.

I glance back at him. Even in the bad light, I can see that his eyes are closed.

"Shit," I say.

Hoping for the best, I reach out and grab the closest leaf. Nothing happens.

Yeah, because poison ivy isn't lightning, Zoe.

I keep holding the leaf and count to ten. No itch.

"Good enough."

More carefully, I pull off the biggest leaf I can find. I tuck it into my palm and tip the water from the other leaves into it. It's not much, but it'll have to do. I hurry back to Vic. His eyes are still closed, but he lets out a breath when I get close.

"Go ahead," he says. "Do your worst."

"Lift up your shirt again," I reply.

He shifts and does what I asked, and I can't help but notice that his cut looks even worse than before.

"Dude," I mutter.

Vic finally opens his eyes. "What?"

I avoid answering him. "Just hold still so I don't poke you by accident."

Gently I pour the water onto his wound. Vic winces hard. His eyes close again, and his breathing whistles in and out.

"Sorry," I say softly.

"It's fine."

"Hang on. I've gotta get a bit more water."

I hop up and repeat my actions three more times before I'm satisfied that the cut is clean. Well. Clean enough. And that'll have to do.

"How does it look?" Vic asks when I'm done.

"Better now that most of the blood is gone," I reply.

It's the truth. It's not so...messy. But it needs something more. Proper antiseptic. Stitches, probably.

Vic doesn't look down to check. He just drops his shirt and leans back against the inside of the stump.

"Why are you being nice to me?" he asks.

"Because in general I'm a nice person," I tell him.

"Not to me," he says.

"Yeah, well. Maybe you should be wondering why *that's* true."

I sit down beside him, because where else am I gonna go? It's not so bad, though. And at least it's warmer.

Vic is quiet for so long that I think he's fallen asleep. I don't bug him because he needs the rest.

But just when I'm about to close my own eyes for a few minutes, he speaks up again.

"Is this gonna..." He trails off and swallows and tries again. "Is it gonna make things worse for your insulin or whatever?"

Now he cares?

"We can take a few minutes," I tell him.

Vic's whole body seems to release a sigh. His shoulders drops, and his jaw loosens. He opens his eyes again too. He meets my gaze.

"Thanks, Zoe," he says.

I fake a scoff. "It's not for *your* sake."

"No?"

"No, you Giant Turd."

A smile ghosts over his lips. "I haven't heard that insult in a long time."

A pang of regret hits me.

What if we'd stayed friends? I wonder before I can stop myself. *Would we have retired Giant*

Turd? Would we have shortened it to GT? Found something new?

I swallow a lump in my throat. "My *point* is that I'm tired too."

To prove it, I do close my eyes now. I can feel Vic watching me. I squeeze my eyes tighter. I slow my breathing too.

"See?" My yawn isn't even fake. "Tired."

But my little plan backfires. I *am* tired. Before I can stop myself, I drift off to sleep for real. And the next thing I know, I'm yanked awake by some sound.

My eyes fly open. It's almost pitch black out.

"Vic?" I gasp.

But a bright yellow stare—not human—is glowing back at me, piercing the dark and making my heart thump.

Chapter Nine

Panic rushes through me. I'm so scared that I can hardly see. My body wants to stand up and run as fast and far away as it can. Then Vic's voice cuts through the fear.

"Don't run," he says.

I realize that I'm already halfway to standing up. I freeze where I am, stuck in some weird squat.

"I read somewhere that wolves like to chase their prey," Vic adds.

A wolf. Yes, that's exactly what's staring at me in the dark. *Damn.*

But I manage to answer Vic in a whisper. "Did you read that on the internet? Because everything there is true. Or so I hear."

"Hilarious, Zoe," he says. "Stay there."

I hear him shift a little, but I don't dare turn and look. I'm afraid to break eye contact with the wolf.

Suddenly Vic is in front of me. He's got his arms out wide, and he lets out the loudest yell I've ever heard in my life.

"Arrrrrrrrrrrrrrrrrrrrrrrrrrr!"

The sound echoes through the woods.

I'm still frozen in the squat, but my mouth is hanging open. Then, about as chill as can be, the wolf walks away. His big gray body slides between the trees until he's gone.

Vic stays where he is, his pose the same. Arms wide open. Legs wide too. It strikes me as funny. A laugh builds up in my chest, then bursts out of my mouth. And once I start, I can't stop. I laugh so hard that I fall to my knees, weird squat forgotten. My stomach hurts from laughing so hard. I even start to cry. When I look over at Vic, he's laughing too. He sinks to the ground, and we both stay that way for a while. Every time one of us stops laughing, we meet each other's eyes, and we laugh all over again.

"Shit," Vic finally says. "That was scary."

"Did you pee your pants?" I reply.

"I don't think so."

"Wait. What? You don't *think* so?"

He shrugs. "My pants are soaked. Could be from sitting on the ground. Could be from pee. I can't tell."

"Ew, Vic," I say, wrinkling my nose. "That's gross."

He flashes a grin, and for a few seconds a memory takes over my brain. Vic and I were five years old, and we were in my backyard. I was wearing a long dress. It was actually my mom's, and I'd snuck it out of her closet. Vic had a tie on over his race-car T-shirt. We were about to have a wedding. One of those things little kids do, you know?

I started to walk up to the spot where he was waiting, and I tripped. He had that same look on his face. A big smile at my expense. And instead of being all sad about it, I'd hopped up and knocked him into the mud. Not because I was pissed off. Because it made us the same.

Why am I thinking about that now? We're not the same at all.

But maybe I miss the times when we were. Just a tiny bit. I'm sure as hell not going admit that to Vic, though.

"Tell me what will happen," he says now.

I don't have to ask him what he means. I know he's talking about my diabetes and my insulin pump.

I hesitate. "Are you sure?"

"I should probably know how to fix you if things go wrong."

"Well, I hate to break it to you, but if a ton of scientists can't fix diabetes, then you can't do it either."

He makes a face. "Look, all I want to know is what to do if you pass out or something. Like, is it worth my time to haul you off the mountain? Or are you gonna die anyway, so I shouldn't bother?"

"Turd," I reply.

"*Giant* Turd," he corrects. "With capital letters. And you should be nicer to the guy who might become your pack mule."

I sigh and pull my pump from my pocket. I immediately forget what I'm about to do. The time glares up at me. We were asleep for two whole hours. *Jesus. I have* got *to get better at being stranded.*

"Zoe?" Vic says.

I make myself swallow down the panic. I hold out the pump so he can see the screen, and I point out the important parts. I show him where it reads my blood sugar. I tell him what a good range is and tap the spot that shows how much insulin is left.

"They're in units," I explain. "And this many units is good for about two hours now."

"Two hours," Vic repeats. "Okay. And if we don't get out of here before they run out? What happens then?"

"I'll start to feel sick. Then I'll *get* sick. I could pass out. After that..." I don't finish because hell, maybe I just don't *want* to finish.

It'll take longer than that, I tell myself. *It really will.*

Vic and I lock eyes. He's not smiling at all now. But somehow I think of the fake wedding memory again. We're the same at the moment. We both know that my life is a ticking time bomb.

Chapter Ten

"We should go," Vic says.

We should. Of course we should. It's the most obvious statement in the world. So why am I questioning it? Why am I stalling? Why am I stuffing my pump into my pocket like it's not important right now?

"You should let me look at your cut again first," I say.

Vic nods. "Okay. Sure. But then we go, right?"

"As long as you look all right," I reply.

In my head, I groan. *Seriously, Zoe? You're stalling because you care more about him than you do about your own life? You must have hit your head. There's no other excuse.*

Vic is adjusting his shirt. He has to peel it away from his injury, and I wince. But he just grunts a bit and finishes the job.

"What do you think, Nurse Zoe?" he asks.

I stick out my tongue at him, but it's to cover my worry. My brain is tossing out a string of silent swear words. The cut is bloody again. And it's a bit... *oozy* or something too. Not quite infected. But only because it hasn't had time to collect enough germs.

"It needs to be bandaged up," I say.

"Oh yeah? Have you got a first-aid kit hidden somewhere?" Vic says, like he's trying too hard to sound like it's not a big deal.

I match his tone, also working at sounding like I'm not afraid he's going to bleed to death or something. "You're a serious pain, you know that, right?"

"We all have to be good at something," he says.

"You're good at cars and math," I reply. "You don't need to add anything else."

Vic smiles. "I'm not *quite* as good at math as I was in seventh grade."

I make a face. "I don't believe you. You always said you were going to *teach* math."

"No, you always said I *should*," he corrects. "I just wanted to impress you, so I agreed."

I'm glad it's too dark for him to see my sudden blush. But I'm frowning a little too. I've just always assumed he'd become Mr. Niels, tenth-grade teacher. Not that I've spent a ton of time thinking about Vic over the last five years. I swear. But still. I guess I occasionally picture grown-up Vic standing behind a desk with chalk marks on his pants.

"I'm actually going to work full time with my dad at the shop," he tells me. "He's changing the name to Niels and Son."

He looks so pleased and proud that I can't think

of a single obnoxious response. And his plan *does* make sense. As I think about it, my mental image of grown-up Vic changes. It morphs into one of him leaning into a car engine in jeans and a T-shirt. Which makes me blush even more for some reason.

"What about you?" he asks. "You still planning on going to Italy for the summer?"

I'm confused for a second. How does he know? Then I remember that he was with me when I first had the idea. It was only a month or so before I found out about my diabetes. I'd just seen a documentary about Rome or something. I'd asked Vic to come with me. It'd seemed impossible that he wouldn't be there. Now, unexpectedly, it seems that way again. I almost—*almost*—ask him if he's still interested. I can picture us in a café, drinking espresso. But he saves me from embarrassing myself by shifting on the ground just then. His teeth clench in visible pain.

Crap, Zoe. Focus!

Thankfully, something comes to me right away.

"Close your eyes," I order. "I have an idea."

"What?"

"Just do it."

I wait until his eyes are closed, then wave my hand in front of his face to be *extra* sure he can't see. When he doesn't react, I unzip my hoodie. The cold air shoots through me. I shiver hard, but I make myself keep going. I slide the hoodie off and yank up the tank top I'm wearing underneath it. My teeth bang together.

"What the hell are you doing?" Vic asks.

I look over. He's opened his eyes.

"Do you have a *tattoo*?" he adds.

I clap a hand over the left side of my chest to cover the ink. Then I realize I've basically left my right boob exposed, so I clap my other hand over that side.

"Dude," I say. "Close. Your. Eyes."

He shrugs and does it, but it's too late. Vic Niels has seen me in my bra. And I thought the car accident and low insulin were bad. But nope. This is worse.

"If you tell anyone about this, I'll murder you in your sleep," I tell him.

"Why wait that long?" he replies. "Just kill me now."

I roll my eyes even though he can't see it. "Keep it up, and I might."

In the dark, I see his lips curve into a smile. But I'm already refocusing. I put the edge of my tank top between my teeth, then pull as hard as I can. Honestly, I must not have been expecting it to work because when it rips, I yelp.

Of course, that makes Vic open his eyes again. "What the hell?"

I don't bother to cover up this time. I'm too cold to care. I finish turning my shirt into a long strip of fabric, then lean closer to Vic.

"Sit up and lift your shirt again," I say.

"You're seriously bossy, you know that?" he replies.

"Keep calling me bossy while I'm bandaging you up," I say. "I dare you."

He smiles again, but his mouth stays closed while I wrap the torn-up shirt around his body. I stretch it enough that I can do it twice. The fit is probably tight, but hopefully that will help stop the bleeding. God, I hope it does.

The second I'm done, I put my hoodie back on and rub my arms, trying to warm up.

"Okay?" I ask Vic.

"Better than ever," he says. "And about that tattoo..."

"You won't let it go, will you?" I say.

"Probably not. But we can walk and talk."

He grabs the side of the tree trunk and uses it to pull himself to his feet. I sigh and do the same thing. My body still hurts. But between my low insulin level and Vic's big cut, I'm putting that at the bottom of my list of important things.

We start off into the woods—*super* slowly—and Vic asks about my ink three more times before I finally answer.

"It's a diabetes ribbon," I say.

He's going to tell me it's ridiculous, I just know it. He's going to totally make fun of it and say I'm obsessed. But I'm allowed to have stuff that means something to me. And so what if it's kind of a boring tattoo? It's mine, and I like it just fine.

"Your mom let you do that?" he asks instead.

I blink, surprised by the question. "She got the same one, actually."

"My mom would lose it," Vic replies. "Remember that time you drew a shooting star on my arm and it wouldn't come off?"

I look away. I don't know why, but I pretend I have zero clue what he's talking about. Like I wasn't thinking just a while ago about us being ten years old and wanting matching tattoos.

"I did that?" I ask. "So weird."

"How can you not remember?" he asks. "It's like a core memory for me."

"I guess I have more important things to think about," I say.

"Yeah, well. That was important to me," he replies.

Oh yeah? If it was so important, then why did you ditch me in seventh grade? Why did you start treating me like I didn't exist and make new *best friends?*

"It wasn't a shooting star," I say after a second. "It was a comet."

"What's the difference?" Vic asks.

I don't want to answer him. It's cheese on top of more cheese. Cheddar with a side of Swiss.

"A comet lasts a while," I say.

"Um...what?" Vic replies.

"You see a shooting star one time, then it's gone. You can see a comet for days."

"Oh."

"Yeah."

I keep my eyes forward, and I'm glad that our hike gets harder right then. It means we're too focused to talk. The ground is rocky and unstable. The trees are thick, and it's so dark that I wonder if we're more lost than when we started.

I look over at Vic. He's limping. His forehead is sweaty. Even in the dark, I can tell that his eyes are glassy too.

"Come *on*, man," I say. "Are you *ever* going to be honest with me?"

"What did I do now?" he replies.

But right after he asks the question, he has to grab a tree to stop himself from falling over.

Chapter Eleven

I want to ease my fear. Vic's too. Maybe make a joke about him being clumsy. Or lazy. Maybe both. *Need a tree to hold you up, slacker?* But the words stick in my throat because I can see that what he really is, is weak. No way can he keep going. Not like this.

"We have to stop again for a bit," I say.

"We can't," he replies.

"I wasn't asking for your opinion."

"Of course you weren't."

“You need to rest,” I tell him.

“I’m not tired,” he says. “I’m just hungry because someone ate my only protein bar.”

I blow out a frustrated breath. Like, ten minutes ago, things seemed almost *normal* between us.

“Are you trying to make me feel like garbage?” I ask.

“No.” Vic sounds like an angry toddler.

Why doesn’t he just stomp his foot? But I answer my own silent question as soon as it pops into my head. *Because he’s too hurt to stomp his foot, Zoe.*

I dig deep into my bucket of niceness and say, “Look, neither of us wants to stop, okay? But we might have to move up the mountain in stages.”

He meets my eyes. “We both know that you can keep going just fine. It’s *me* that’s the problem.”

I clue in. He’s not trying to make me feel bad. *He* feels bad. Now, ironically, *I* feel bad too.

"Sit down," I order abruptly. "Don't move an inch. I'm going to try to find you something to eat, and if that doesn't work, both of us will know you're a big fat liar about being hungry."

I spin away. If I move fast, maybe Vic won't figure out it's a trick to get him to rest. But he calls out anyway.

"Hey, Zoe?" he says.

I'm not far enough away to pretend I don't hear him, so I sigh and turn back. "What, Vic?"

"Think you can find me a pizza?" He gives me a weak smile and plunks to the ground.

I make a face. "You're the worst."

But really I'm worried. Not just because I don't want him to die but because it's starting to feel like we *actually* might not make it.

A lump digs into my throat, and I kick the rocks in front of me. I would've been better off failing English than doing this. And I mean, really. Screw my trip to Italy. Screw my plans for anything. What were the chances that in a situation like this, it'd be me, the T1D, who was doing better?

I don't see anything close to edible either.

What did you think would happen, Zoe? That you really would *find a pizza?*

But a second later when I take another step forward, I'm in a small clearing. The moon makes a brief appearance above me, and its dull light reveals a patch of bright pink nestled in green leaves.

Salmonberries. Yes!

"Score," I say under my breath.

They're probably the one wild berry I recognize.

Forgetting that the search was a trick to stall Vic, I hold out the bottom of my hoodie and fill it with every salmonberry in sight. Once that's done, I make my way back to him. He hasn't moved. Part of me is happy because just this once, he listened. But another part of me—maybe a bigger one—is even more worried than I was a minute ago. The Vic I know—or *knew*—would be complaining about being stuck there. *This* Vic has closed his eyes and is sitting too still.

This isn't good.

"Hey," I say, somehow managing to keep my voice steady. "No pizza. But I got you some dessert."

Vic opens his eyes, and relief hits me like a truck. I sit down next to him and aim my berry-filled hoodie in his direction.

"I'm giving you the lint for no extra charge," I tell him.

"Thoughtful," he replies.

He goes quiet again, stuffing the berries into his mouth. My stomach rumbles.

"You want some?" Vic asks.

As if in reply, my insulin pump alarms me to a rising high. Which is not awesome. And which also reminds me that I shouldn't eat even if I want to. Not enough insulin to cover a damn bite.

“I’m good,” I lie. “Ate your protein bar, remember?”

My pump alarms again, and I silence it.

“Zoe...” Vic says.

I tense for a comment about my diabetes.

“I’m sorry,” he says instead.

My throat gets scratchy, and I have to clear it before answering him. “It was just an accident.”

“What was?” he asks, sounding confused.

“Uh, the accident was an accident,” I tell him, sounding just as puzzled.

“I’m not sorry for the accident.” He pauses. “I mean, I *am* sorry for that. But it’s not what I’m talking about.”

I stare at him. Am *I* confused? Or is *he* confused?

He closes his eyes again. It’s gotta be him.

“Vic?” I say after a long second of silence.

“Mmph,” he mumbles.

“Are you gonna tell me what you’re talking about?” I ask.

His eyelids flutter, then lift, and he meets my stare. "I'm trying to say sorry for almost killing you when you first found out you were diabetic."

What does he mean?

I start to ask him, but his head droops, and I know he's in even bigger trouble than I thought.

Chapter Twelve

I grab Vic's arm and say his name. He doesn't answer, so I give him a small shake.

"Vic," I say. "You need to stay with me."

He still doesn't answer.

"Vic. Please."

I lean in closer and put my hand on his chest. It's moving in and out. He's breathing.

"Thank the sweet baby Jesus," I mutter.

But my heart isn't in the relieved words. Sure,

Vic's alive. Wonderful. Except for the part where he's passed out.

In my head, I hear his voice. *We both know I'm the problem.*

Yesterday I would've paid for him to say that, even out of context like this. But right now it makes my heart thump louder than a bongo drum. What if Vic is right? What if I'm the only one of us who can keep going? Then what? I could leave. Try to get help and come back.

But what if he dies while I'm gone?

"Vic," I say loudly. "I need you to wake up. Don't you want to tell me how you almost killed me?"

I get no response.

"Dammit, Vic!"

I close my eyes. Tears burn hot underneath my eyelids. And my insulin pump blares an alarm because of course it does.

"Fuck you too," I say to it.

But I yank it out anyway. Its little screen is lit up with not one but two warnings. The first is about low insulin. The second is about my high blood sugar, which is almost three times the level it should be.

As if I need to be told.

I'm so thirsty that it hurts. My stomach is tossing around too. Both clear signs of the rise in blood sugar. I'm probably even higher than the pump says because it's usually fifteen or so minutes behind. It's only going to get worse. I should be giving myself a solid dose of insulin, but I'm afraid to use even one unit. I stuff the pump away again.

"Vic?" I say for the millionth time.

Think, Zoe. There has to be a way out of this.

But before my brain can kick out a single idea, a weird noise cuts through the night air.

Thud-thud. Thud-thud.

It's faint but getting louder. It's also above me.

Then I realize that I *know* the sound. It's a helicopter.

"Holy shit," I breathe.

Vic mumbles something, but I can't waste time figuring out what it is. The helicopter is getting closer. I can see its lights.

They're looking for us. They have to be.

I jerk into action, pushing to my feet, then waving my hands over my head and yelling.

"Down here!" I call out. "We're down here!"

What am I doing?

They obviously can't hear me. I can't hear *myself* over the helicopter noise. The tree cover is too thick for them to see me, too, even with their spotlights.

I fling a look around. I need higher ground. I could climb a tree or—

There!

It looks like a sloped boulder. It's kind of far away, and visible only because of the helicopter's lights. But if I can get there and get to the top, maybe I stand a chance of being seen. I take off running. And I'm yelling again even though it won't do any damn good.

"Wait! Hey! Come on, you tools! *Wait*!"

The helicopter's lights aren't helping me anymore. It's facing the other direction. Where *is* that boulder? I feel like I'm lost. But I'm also in the open now, and the helicopter hovers in the air for a few seconds.

Hope fills me. *They see me!* I stop where I am, breathing heavily. And then my hope falls away. The helicopter is on the move.

No, no, no!

"Hey!" I scream. "*Hey*!"

There's no chance in hell I can catch it. But I run again anyway. Faster and faster, I go. My boots smack into the ground.

"Wait!" I yell.

I'm crying. Sweating. My eyes sting. The churn in my gut is horrible. And the worst thing is that no matter how hard I try, I'm never going to be as fast as a helicopter. I keep moving for another few seconds anyway. Just long enough for the *thud-thud, thud-thud* of the helicopter to fade.

This time when I holler, it's nothing more than a wordless "Ahhhhhhhhhh!"

I let it out until my throat hurts, but it's not good enough. I want to sink down, curl into a ball and close my eyes. In fact, I want anything other than to be right here, right now. And for some reason, I blame this whole thing on my seventh-grade teacher. The one who wanted that essay about what we'd do if we were lost in the wilderness.

Come on, Zoe. Be reasonable.

"Reasonable how?" I ask myself out loud. "It's *un*reasonable to ask me to be reasonable. How would I survive? I wouldn't, remember?"

But really, there's only one thing I can do anyway. I have to stop and turn around. I need to get back to Vic before I'm so lost that I *can't* find my way back to him.

For an extra-long second, I stare up at the dark sky. I'm not ashamed to admit that I'm hoping if I want it bad enough, the helicopter will come back. It doesn't. Why would it? Clearly, my control over the universe is lacking.

Bitterly, I spin and take a step. Except instead of landing on solid ground, my foot hits nothing but air. My arms flail. I topple backward. My butt hits the dirt in a way that makes me slide forward, and I'm suddenly hanging on the edge of a steep drop. My feet are *dangling.* And below me I can just barely see that at the bottom is a river.

Blood rushes through my head. My instinct is to scramble back. But if I move an inch in the wrong direction, I'm sure I'll plunge to my death down the side of the mountain.

Chapter Thirteen

I hold very, very still.

I breathe in.

I breathe out.

I hold even more still. I'm a statue.

But I have to move. *Have to.* Because underneath me, I can feel pebbles falling away. Worse, I can hear them. *Plink, plink.* And is that a splash? It can't be. But it's almost like the ground *wants* to slide down to the river, taking me with it.

Swallowing, I stretch my arms back and press my hands down. The dirt is cold and slippery under my fingers. It feels anything but good, and I swallow again. I make myself try to find something to grab. A proper rock. A branch. Hell, a patch of grass would work. But there's nothing. Just the dirt and the death wish it has for me.

I lift up my left hand, intending to widen my search. It's a mistake. I slide a bit farther forward. I'm going to go over. I can feel it, and I can't stop it. But just as the world starts to drop out from under me, something yanks me back to safety.

"Zoe." It's Vic.

Where did he come from? Scratch that question. I don't *care* where he came from. I care only that he's there. He's got his hands under my arms. My back is pressed to his chest. And I've never, not in my whole life, been so happy to be held tightly by a person I hate.

Do you really hate him?

"No," I mumble.

Of course I don't. I never have. I've just been *hurt.*

Such a great time to realize it, right?

"Zoe?" Vic says.

"I don't hate you," I tell him.

"Gee, thanks," he replies.

I don't say anything else for a long minute. I'm thinking about the sleepovers we had when we were kids. Hiding in our blanket fort. Trash-talking a girl named Sally because she called us boyfriend and girlfriend.

Zoe and Vic, sitting in a tree...K-I-S-S-I-N-G.

That was before our actual kiss. Which, for the record, did *not* happen in a tree. We were in my backyard, sitting on my old swing set. And it was Vic's idea. He told me he'd been thinking about it, and it made sense. A practice kiss, he'd called it. Better to try it out with each other than to mess it up on a date or something. But the truth is, the second it happened, it stopped being practice. At least for me.

Of course, I never told that to Vic. So I don't know why I feel like telling him now. I *really* don't know why I have to bite my lip to stop myself from blurting it out.

I hate that we stopped being friends. That's what I actually hate.

Maybe I blamed myself for liking him like that. And maybe I've never let that go.

My throat is doing the scratchy want-to-cry thing again. I have *got* to get myself together. I've cried more in the last day than I've cried in the last year.

I start to move away from Vic. Then I remember the last bit of our conversation before he passed out.

"Hey, Vic," I blurt out. "What did you mean when you said you were sorry for trying to kill me?"

He groans. "Did I tell you that?"

"Uh, yeah. Yeah, you did, Vic."

"Christ. I must've been in a lot of pain."

I stuff down my sympathy.

"You might as well explain it," I say. "Whatever it is, you don't want to die with it on your conscience."

"Bold of you to assume I have a conscience," he replies.

"I'm serious."

"Yeah, but you *just* stopped hating me."

I adjust my body so I can see his face. But for some reason, I don't fully pull away from him. The closeness is comforting. Also, Vic looks a bit better. His face isn't quite so pale, and his eyes aren't as glassy. Maybe the salmonberries and the rest helped.

"I want to know anyway," I say. "And for the record, I don't think I ever hated you for real. I was just pissed off that you started ignoring me."

He surprises me then. He puts his hand on top of mine, and the tips of his fingers slide between my knuckles. Next I surprise myself. Because I turn my palm up, and our fingers thread together.

"You were my best friend," I tell him.

"I'm sorry, Zoe," Vic says. "And not just because we might die out here, okay? I was a bad friend. Worse than bad." He pauses. "Do you remember my thirteenth birthday?"

I nod. I remember it perfectly. It was about a week after I'd found out about my diabetes. The first time going out on my own, and my mom had been pretty freaked out. It was also the last time we hung out before Vic started being the aforementioned Giant Turd.

"At the amusement park," I say.

"Yeah." He pauses again and clears his throat. "Do you remember how you were thirsty after we rode the big coaster?"

Now I frown. "Sort of."

He laughs, sounding kind of bitter. "Trust me. You were thirsty. You asked me to get you a diet soda."

"Okay?"

"And Bobby White and Luke Chen dared me to get you a regular one instead." Vic runs his hand over his hair and shakes his head. "I'm sorry, Zoe. So sorry. Those guys...they made fun of me all the time. Teased me about having a girlfriend. I know now that they were jealous. But back then...whatever. It's not a good excuse. If I'm being honest, I would *rather* have had you as my girlfriend."

He'd wanted me to be his girlfriend? My face feels warm. So do my insides. I almost forget that he's just confessed to thinking he'd fed me a sugary death. I have to force myself to make that part matter.

"Back the truck up here, Vic," I say. "You wanted to murder me with sugar because you liked me more than as a friend?"

His eyes widen. "What? No."

"Good. Because that would be truly messed up."

He liked me.

Vic studies my face. "You're screwing with me, aren't you?"

"Of course I am," I reply. "You were a kid. I just don't get why you didn't tell me about it. Like, why just go straight from *liking* me to ditching me for five entire years?"

"Because after you drank what I gave you, you got sick," he says. "It *scared* me."

I can tell that Vic means all of what he's saying. He really is sorry. He really didn't understand. And he was in seventh grade.

He swallows. "My mom told me I could've killed you. I think she was scared too."

"Vic," I say. "You couldn't have killed me with one sugary soda."

"I know," he states, guilt trickling through the two words.

He knows.

My stomach sinks. Why does that admission seem worse?

"For how long?" I ask.

Vic meets my eyes and licks his lips. "Since about ninth grade."

"Two whole years?" My voice is small.

"For about a year after that, I convinced myself you were better off without me anyway. Who needed a friend like that?"

"I did." It comes out in a whisper. "*I* needed a friend like that. Do you have any idea how hard it was for me?"

"Yes." He sounds like he wants to choke on the word.

"You suck, Vic."

"I wanted to tell you, Zoe," he says. "I went to your house a hundred times. I stood outside and stared at your window. I wrote you letters. Once, before school last year, I stole a shot of my mom's tequila to try and work up enough nerve to talk to you."

I almost want to laugh. But not quite. Vic keeps talking anyway.

"Every time I saw you, I could tell how much you hated me. And I didn't blame you. So I tried to make this...I dunno...*wall*? An emotional one. I leaned into the idea that we were, like, enemies." He pauses. "I do suck. I really do."

I look down so he can't see the tears in my eyes. We're still holding hands, and it should be weird. I've spent a lot of time being nothing but mad at him. My feelings have been so hurt for so long, and we've been talking again for, like, five minutes. Not to mention that we're stuck on the side of this damn mountain, so much closer to death than a full-sugar drink could ever take me. So why isn't the hand-holding weird? Why am I glad about everything? Well, sort of everything. I could do without the death bit, I guess.

I open my mouth to say something, but before I can speak, the ground under us shifts. Whatever's been holding us in place for the last few minutes gives way. And together we go sliding over the edge toward the river below.

Chapter Fourteen

We're caught in a mudslide. And it's not a straight drop down the cliff like I'd thought. It's steep, yes. But also bumpy. Instead of flying through the air, we thump over the rocks and dirt and low-lying shrubs. We twist and turn. But somehow we keep holding hands. Maybe we're lucky we don't break our fingers or our arms because of it. I'm glad anyway. It means that when we hit the river with an icy splash, we don't get separated. Not even when a current kicks up and tosses us hard into the bank on the other side.

For a second I just stay where I am. Clinging hard to Vic's hand. Trying to catch my breath because it feels like I got kicked in the stomach. Then panic hits me.

My insulin pump.

It's not really waterproof. It isn't meant to take a beating like this. And even if I have only *one* unit left in it, I want to make sure I get it.

I free my hand from Vic's and jam it into my soaking-wet pants pocket. The pump is still there. I yank it out and tap its center button. The screen comes to life, and I give it a grateful squeeze before stuffing it away again.

I turn to Vic. "Hey, did you—"

My words die on my lips. Vic's eyes are closed, and his mouth is open. The wrap job I did on his stomach wound has come free. Fresh blood seeps out.

"Fuck. Oh fuck," I say. "Vic?"

I crawl closer, but I'm scared to touch him. Terrified it will reveal what I don't want to know.

"Vic." I sound desperate, but I don't care. "Vic, please wake up."

Nothing happens.

"Come on," I say. "You seriously can't pass out three times. It's not fair."

He doesn't budge.

"Please. If you wake up, I promise I'll forgive you for the soda. For being too chicken to tell me. For *everything.* I swear. I won't even make you beg."

Vic's chest lifts. Slowly. Then it drops. I barely have time to be grateful before he starts shivering. For a full-on panicked second, I wonder if he might be having a seizure. I had one once when I was thirteen. My blood sugar dropped too low, too fast for me to notice. I fainted, then seized.

Could Vic have hit his head hard enough to knock his brain around? But a few heartbeats pass, and I see that his teeth are banging together. His lips are blue.

He's freezing.

Hypothermia isn't any better than a seizure. But at least it's something I can help with.

"Yes," I say under my breath. "I can work with that."

I can also relate. I'm cold too. And the longer I sit there, the worse it gets.

Except I don't move. Because the idea that fills my brain is the worst one I've ever had. It's that thing they do in movies. Body heat. Getting totally naked. Use each other to get warm.

"I can *not* work with *that*," I mutter.

Think, Zoe, think.

But the idea of body heat won't go away. It's like a tattoo in my head. My face is hot from it even though the rest of me is still basically made of ice.

Maybe there's no other choice.

Vic and Zoe, sitting in a tree...

"Shut up," I say.

It might not even work. Maybe we'll just die naked with nothing between us but my insulin pump.

A wild laugh tries to escape from my chest. But it sticks there.

My insulin pump.

A new idea takes over. One that involves keeping my clothes on but taking a different risk.

Slowly I pull the pump from my pocket. Its screen tells me I'm down to my very last bit of insulin.

"I can do this," I tell myself. "I mean...what's the worst that can happen?"

I look over at Vic. He's stopped shivering, but I don't think that's a good thing.

I look back down at my pump. I take a big breath, then press the buttons to tell it to give me the rest of the insulin. I even add two units, just in case there's some extra. When it finishes, it alarms. No surprise. But I'm over it. I give the pump a squeeze, shove it into my pocket, then rush around, collecting bits of dry broken branches. Once I have a pile, I take out my pump again.

"We're going to be okay," I say to it.

I remove it from my body. I feel naked, but I stuff the feeling away. I grab a skinny rock from nearby and use it to open the pump's battery slot. Now the pump loses it with a new alarm. A screeching blare. I ignore it and keep going with my plan.

From my other pocket, I take out the foil gum wrapper. I stare down at it.

This will work. It has to.

In my head I see Mr. Flannigan showing us how to do this. How to make a fire. I follow the instructions just like he explained.

I fold the gum wrapper in half.

I tear out a little piece in the middle of the foil and pinch the opening into a point.

Please work, please work, please work, I chant silently.

Holding my breath, I bend the wrapper. I put one corner onto each end of the battery.

For a long second nothing happens. I'm still holding my breath, and my lungs burn. Then, just when I'm about to give up, a little flame dances to life in the middle of the wrapper.

"Holy shit," I whisper.

I send a thousand apologies to Mr. Flannigan, wherever he is now. But I don't have much time. The tiny fire won't last long.

Carefully I set it down on the nearest rock. I dig into my pocket again, pulling out a wad of pocket lint and old receipts. I start feeding the fire. The lint. The mostly wet receipts. The dry branches I collected. The whole time, I still don't believe it's working. But the flames get bigger. And bigger. And bigger.

Smoke billows up and makes me cough. But it's a good thing. The bigger the fire is, the better. I need the heat for the search-and-rescue equipment

Vic was talking about earlier. I grab some other branches. I add them to the fire too. Soon it's a proper blaze.

Now Vic coughs, and I turn his way. He's sitting up, his hand on his head.

"Zoe?" he says.

If he's going to add anything else, he doesn't get a chance to. Because a *thud-thud, thud-thud* fills the air. We both look toward the sound. The helicopter lights are visible overhead. And they're headed our way.

Chapter Fifteen

After the helicopter gets to us, everything happens in a blur. They check us out and get us loaded up. They take us right to the hospital, landing us on the roof. From there we're sent to two different rooms.

My mom shows up, freaking out. I want to tell her to chill because I'm *alive*, but instead I just cry and hug her.

A nurse hooks me up to an IV. I hook *myself* up to the backup insulin pump my mom brought. My blood sugar is higher than the helicopter was, but I feel okay. No broken bones. Nothing seriously damaged. The doctors are impressed, to be honest. Car crash. Mudslide. Diabetes. I'm a miracle. Ha.

Finally the medical people leave us alone. I expect a lecture from my mom. But she just falls asleep in the big chair beside my bed. I should probably be sleeping too. Instead I quietly lower the rail beside me and climb out.

I've got some experience with IVs from when I was first diagnosed with diabetes. It takes me only a minute to change the settings so I can unplug the IV unit from the wall. I tiptoe past my mom and make my way across the hallway to Vic's room. I stand in the doorway and stare at him. His parents *were* here, but they're not now. Maybe grabbing a coffee or something. His eyes are closed, but after a second he speaks up.

"Take a picture—it'll last longer," he says.

My shoulders sag with relief. "Giant Turd. I saved your life."

"I know. It was very nice of you." Vic laughs, then coughs, then puts his hand on his ribs. "Ouch."

I step into the room and sit on the edge of his bed. "Are you all right?"

"Concussion," he says. "Bruises everywhere. You?"

"Better than you," I reply.

He sticks out his tongue, and it reminds me *hard* of when we were kids. My heart squeezes tight in my chest. The last five years go out of my head, and I lean in and hug him.

"Ouch," Vic repeats.

"Oops," I say. "Sorry."

I start to pull away, but his hand catches mine, and he pulls me back in. I let my body curl up beside his. To be honest, it kinda feels like it belongs there.

"I missed you, Zoe," he tells me.

I can't think of anything sarcastic to say back to him.

Are my feelings still hurt? Of course. The last five years haven't just disappeared. Can I let it go? Maybe not right away. But when he was unconscious, I promised him I'd forgive him if he woke up. I have to make good on that, don't I?

Make excuses much, Zoe?

But I don't care. I *want* to forgive him. Even if it takes a while.

"I missed you too," I admit after another second.

"Can I ask you something?" Vic says.

"Sure," I reply.

I expect him to ask about school. To wonder aloud if things will be weird on Monday. If we'll go back to low-key enemy territory or if we'll suddenly be weird best friends again.

"Do you think we'll still have to write that essay for English?" he asks instead.

I laugh. But my brain goes back to the original essay. The seventh-grade one about how we'd survive if we got stranded on an island. I think about my answer. *I wouldn't.* Would it change now? I mean, my diabetes hasn't magically disappeared. I'd still die without my insulin. But maybe I'd think about my answer a bit more. And maybe if we *do* have to write the final essay for English, I'll find something better to say. Something not too cringey. But also something true. Like how my diabetes is part of me, but it isn't the only thing I am. Or how my insulin pump keeps me alive every day and how having it with me saved my life on the mountain in a different way. Or maybe just how frustrating it is that people don't understand it. Vic's mom, for example. He couldn't *really* have killed me with one sugary soda. If she'd known that and had explained it to him, we might still be friends. We might have stayed friends all this time. I dunno. I'll have to think about it more. But in any case, the essay doesn't seem so awful anymore.

I must be quiet for too long, because Vic gives me a little nudge.

"Zoe?" he says. "Did you fall asleep?"

I tip my head up to look at him. Vic's expression is...*funny.* It's like...serious. But embarrassed at the same time. I frown, trying to make sense of it. Then I see his eyes lower. He's staring at my lips. And I clue in.

He wants to kiss me.

And even if I'm not sure about any other damn thing, I know for sure that I want to kiss him back.

So I do.

Melinda Di Lorenzo has been writing professionally for more than a decade and is the author of *Counting Scars*, *Racing Hearts*, *Normal Kids* and *The Truth About Maura* in the Orca Soundings line. She is the bestselling author of more than 30 books. Melinda lives in the Lower Mainland region of BC, where she finds plenty of inspiration.

For more information on Type 1 Diabetes
please visit www.jdrf.ca